The "Haab"

onth Names

tree

"maw" or great mouth
and eyes of the earth

he scattered

Uayeb

monkey

conch shell and feather

Pop

the first
girl and boy

North Chac

corn seed

mature corn

East Chac

making rope

Cumhu

storm

building

Kayab

Uo

emerge

Corn God

rodent

she is

Pax

Zip

daybreak

black storm
and death

ear of corn

young corn

jaguar

lady

Zotz

fire

moon

Muan

West Chac

turtle

Kaukin

house

growing corn people

South Chac

deer

rain

celestial two-headed dragon staff

earth

Mac

Tzec

Xul

Yaykin

Mol

Chen

Yax

Zac

Ceh

Lilli's

WHY THERE IS NO ARGUING IN HEAVEN

A *Mayan Myth*

DEBORAH NOURSE LATTIMORE

HARPER & ROW, PUBLISHERS

For my sisters,
Marthermarie and Melanie

Why There Is No Arguing in Heaven
Copyright © 1989 by Deborah Nourse Lattimore
Printed in the U.S.A. All rights reserved.
Typography by Andrew Rhodes
1   2   3   4   5   6   7   8   9   10
First Edition

Library of Congress Cataloging-in-Publication Data
Lattimore, Deborah Nourse.
    Why there is no arguing in heaven : a Mayan myth / by Deborah Nourse
Lattimore. — 1st ed.
        p.   cm.
    Summary: Hunab Ku, the first Creator God of the Mayas, challenges the
Moon Goddess and Lizard House to create a being to worship him, but the
Maize God succeeds where the others fail.
    ISBN 0-06-023717-1 : $
    ISBN 0-06-023718-X (lib. bdg.) : $
    1. Mayas—Legends.   2. Mayas—Religion and mythology—Juvenile
literature.   3. Indians of Mexico—Religion and mythology—Juvenile
literature.   4. Indians of Mexico—Legends.   5. Indians of Central
America—Legends.   6. Indians of Central America—Religion and
mythology—Juvenile literature.   [1. Mayas—Legends.   2. Indians of
Central America—Legends.]   I. Title.
F1435.3.F6L37 1989
398.2'09728—dc19   87-35045
[E]   CIP
                                                             AC

Before there was the world, darkness was all that was. There were no people, no stones or trees, no grass, and no land. Just the all-night was there. In this darkness on a throne surrounded by shining *ceiba* trees sat Hunab Ku, the first Creator God. At his feet sat the other gods. The Sun God was quiet. The Maize God was watchful. But Lizard House and the Moon Goddess argued as to which of the gods was greatest after Hunab Ku.

"A great god is one who creates, not one who argues," said Hunab Ku.
He took a jar of water from the Rain Gods and spat into it. Then he
poured it down through the darkness, stirring it with his finger.
"Let my creation show its face," said Hunab Ku.

As he spoke, it happened. Earth rose. Forests grew, and flowers
blossomed. The Sun God filled the skies with yellow light. With his
finger Hunab Ku drew a line through the earth. Deer and birds, snakes
and jaguars sprang up. They flew and leapt and wriggled across the four
directions.

"Let your sounds fill the air!" Hunab Ku said to all the animals. "Worship us!"

But hissing, warbling, cawing, crying, and screeching was all Hunab Ku heard.

"What a terrible noise!" exclaimed Hunab Ku.

He swept his staff from east to west through the clouds. The animals scattered off to the lakes, the forests, and the mountains. Lizard House and the Moon Goddess argued again, while the Maize God watched and listened and said nothing.

"Stop!" said Hunab Ku. TZAM! went his staff as it struck the floor of heaven. "Whoever can create a being worthy of worshipping us will be the second greatest god after me and will have the honor of sitting at my side."

"Let my creation please you," said Lizard House. He reached down and scooped up the fresh, moist earth and gave it to Hunab Ku.

"Use *this*." Hunab Ku took the earth and fashioned a man. He spat life into it and put it down.

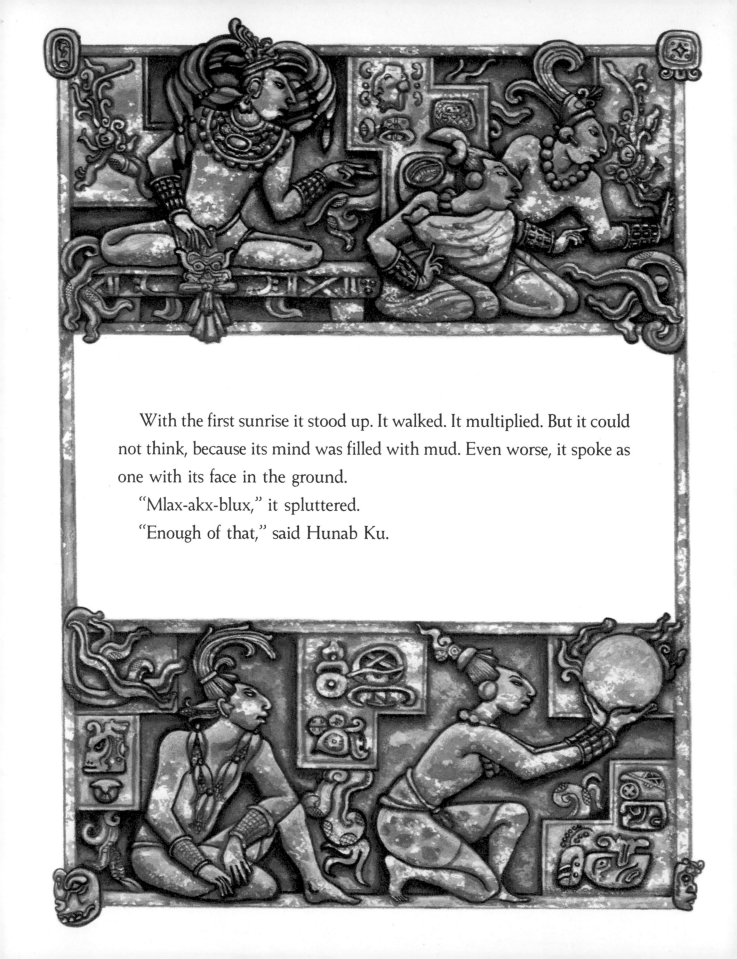

With the first sunrise it stood up. It walked. It multiplied. But it could not think, because its mind was filled with mud. Even worse, it spoke as one with its face in the ground.

"Mlax-akx-blux," it spluttered.

"Enough of that," said Hunab Ku.

He waved to the Rain Gods. Down from the four corners of the sky cascaded the all-washing water of the Rain Gods, the Chacs, and flooded the earth. The mud men tried to run, but the water found them and they melted away. Only a puddle remained, and it became a deep pool, a *cenote*. The Moon Goddess rocked with laughter.

But the Maize God quietly took the last lump of mud and put it in his pouch.

The Moon Goddess pulled a *catzim* tree from its roots and gave it to Hunab Ku. "*Here* is your worshipper," she said.

Hunab Ku twisted the boughs to look like a man. He spat life into it and set it down. Soon the Sun God rose in the sky.

The wood man stood up. It walked. It multiplied. Soon there were many wood men. They cooked and hunted and made homes.

"Men of wood," called out Hunab Ku. "Worship us, your creators."

The wood men stood still and blinked at the sun. "Kab-kac-kac-TZREEEK-TZREEEK, kab-kac-kac-TZREEEK-TZREEEK," they screeched. Their words grated together like cricket legs.

"No good," said Hunab Ku. "They speak like twigs. They move like planting sticks. They think like stones. And they do not worship us."

Again Hunab Ku raised his staff to the Chacs. Swiftly their flood struck the wood men. Grinding stones broke some into splinters. Others became charcoal in their own cooking fires. Those few who escaped climbed trees and became monkeys.

The last stick the Maize God took and quietly put in his pouch.

"I have seen enough," said Hunab Ku. "No one will sit at my side."

Just as Hunab Ku raised his staff to destroy the world below, the Maize God stood up.

"Wait," he cried. "The spirits of men deserve better than mud or wood. Let me plant my seeds, and you can see for yourself."

"I tire of poor creations," said Hunab Ku. "Let Lizard House and the Moon Goddess go to the earth and test these spirits of yours. If they are as you say, you may plant your seeds."

Now, if there is one thing a god does not like to do, it is to leave Heaven. Only the Maize God likes the earth, for that is where his magic works its wonders. So Lizard House and the Moon Goddess were angry.

"We will soon rid ourselves of these spirits," they muttered, and descended to earth.

The Maize God clapped his hands, and from between his fingers two flowing forms appeared. They were the spirits of men. They floated down until they stood before Lizard House and the Moon Goddess.

"If you are worthy enough to be men," said the Moon Goddess to the spirits, "you must enter the House of the Chacs and thank them for the water that made this earth. We will await you."

The spirits bowed their heads and entered the House of the Chacs. *Bang!* The door slammed shut and fastened itself. Inside, a terrible storm brewed. But the spirits spread themselves against the walls like a cloud forest above the mountains of Lake Atitlàn.

Lizard House and the Moon Goddess laughed with delight.

"If these are the spirits of leftover mud men," said the Moon Goddess, "they will surely wash away, and we can return to Heaven."

Yet at daybreak the spirits appeared, unharmed.

The Moon Goddess growled and stamped her foot. But Lizard House smiled.

"Poor spirits," he said. "You look cold. Take these hollow sticks of fat pine to the House of Gloom and warm yourselves with their fire. But return these as you found them. They belong to gods."

The respectful spirits entered the House of Gloom. *Bang!* The door slammed shut and fastened itself. Inside, the air was thicker and darker than smoke in the shrine of death. But the spirits put fireflies into the sticks of fat pine and waved them around.

"Ha!" laughed Lizard House. "See the lights! If these are the spirits of leftover wood men, they will burn up, and we can return to Heaven."

As the yellow light filled the morning sky, the spirits once again appeared. In their hands were the sticks of fat pine, untouched.

"These clever spirits have passed your tests," said Hunab Ku, who had been watching.

"Not all of them!" said Lizard House and the Moon Goddess. They seized the two spirits and threw them into the nearby river.

TZAM! The mighty staff of Hunab Ku struck the floor of heaven. He pointed at Lizard House.

"For this deed," he thundered, "mud shall be your throne. And Moon Goddess, trees shall cover your face as you roam the endless night sky. Come, Maize God. Sow your seeds."

The Maize God knew that the river would rise and that the spirits were not lost. He opened his pouch and spread the wet earth flat and even. With his stick he made holes. Into the holes he poured grains of maize. Hunab Ku spat life into them. Then the river, filled with the spirits of men, flowed onto the earth.

Before their eyes the gods saw a race of tall, bronze men and women spring up. They walked and made houses of mud and wood. They toiled in the fields and hunted animals.

Then they knelt before the gods and spoke with a voice like the song of a turtledove flying above rippling waters.

"Because of all the gods of water and earth, trees and land, sky, sun, and moon, we were created. We worship you."

Hunab Ku was filled with a gladness that spread from the shining *ceiba* trees to the corners of the sky. And every spring, when the new corn showed its golden bounty, the Maize God quietly took his place beside Hunab Ku.

In Heaven, from that day to this, there has been no arguing.

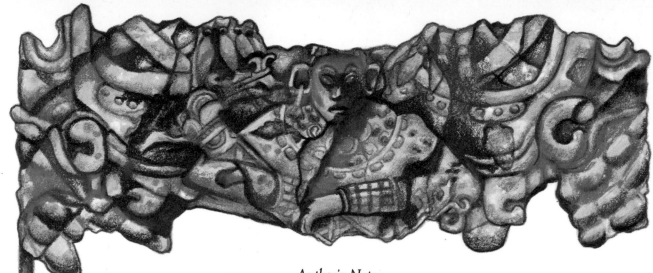

Author's Note

In the early 1500s the Mayan Indians of Guatemala discovered that strange bearded men called Spaniards had invaded Mexico. They also learned that these men had killed many people, attacked sacred temples with fire tubes called cannons, and burned all the holy writings. Quickly, they gathered their own history in bundles of codices, or books painted on plastered wood bark or deerskin. Courageous foot runners carried them over the steep volcanic mountains to Chichicastenango and hid them. One hundred fifty years later a Spanish priest, Padre Ximénez, found one of these books, the *Popol Vuh*. His love of learning and knowledge of the Mayan language, Quiché, prompted him to translate the book. To his delight he found that in his hands was the first history of the Mayan world, its creation, and the myths of the gods. But like many early translators, Padre Ximénez added elements of his own time, and the original story was altered.

The stories of the Maya have been translated many times since, and the ancient voices seem very far away. When I began to read about the creation of the world and man, I found that in dozens of different interpretations several gods and ideas appeared again and again. Taking these elements and putting them together with the designs I found in the stonework and painted art, I have tried to present the most straightforward version of the first Mayan creation story. It is my hope that this version can impart the spirit of the Maya, a beautiful and enduring race living in Guatemala and parts of Mexico among the forests of shining *ceiba* trees.

D.N.L.

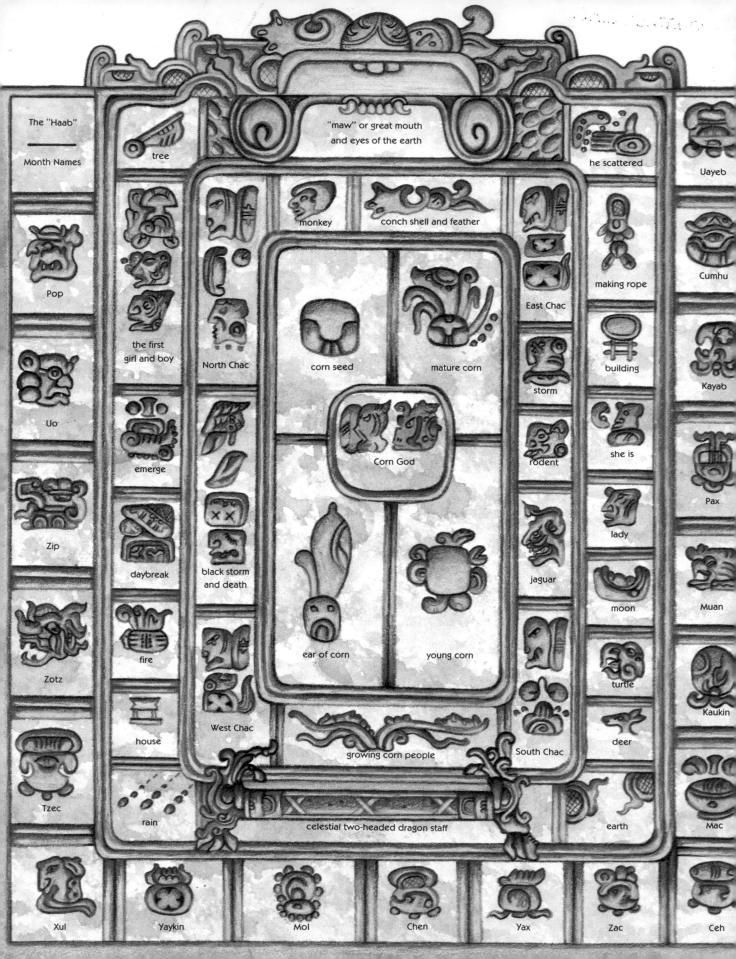

The "Haab"

Month Names

tree

"maw" or great mouth
and eyes of the earth

he scattered

Uayeb

Pop

monkey

conch shell and feather

making rope

Cumhu

the first
girl and boy

North Chac

corn seed

mature corn

East Chac

building

Kayab

Uo

storm

she is

emerge

Corn God

rodent

lady

Pax

Zip

daybreak

black storm
and death

jaguar

moon

Muan

Zotz

fire

turtle

Kaukin

West Chac

house

ear of corn

young corn

South Chac

deer

earth

Mac

Tzec

rain

growing corn people

celestial two-headed dragon staff

Xul

Yaykin

Mol

Chen

Yax

Zac

Ceh